# HILDA HEN'S
# HAPPY BIRTHDAY

**For Lucy and Graham**

# HILDA HEN'S HAPPY BIRTHDAY

**Mary Wormell**

**GOLLANCZ CHILDREN'S PAPERBACKS**
LONDON

It was a lovely sunny morning and Hilda Hen
wondered if anyone had remembered that
it was her birthday.
First she went to the horse's stable.

"Just look," clucked Hilda.
"Folly, the horse, has left me
some oats. How nice."
She quickly gobbled them up.

The horse arrived back from her morning gallop.
"Oh, the oats!" snorted the horse.
"Lovely," clucked Hilda.
"Thank you so much."

And she went on her way.

"Just look," clucked Hilda.
"The gardener has left me
some apples. Yum-yum."

She eagerly pecked at the apples.

The gardener looked down.
"Oh, the apples," she sighed.
"Lovely," clucked Hilda.
"Thank you so much."

And she went on her way.

"Just look," clucked Hilda.
"The farmer's wife has made me
a dust bath. How kind."

**She hurriedly scraped the flowers
out of the way.**

The farmer's wife arrived with her
watering can.
"Oh, the flower bed," she wailed.
"Lovely," clucked Hilda.
"Thank you so much."

And she went on her way.

"Just look," clucked Hilda.
"The farmer has left me some
tea and biscuits. My favourites."

She happily drank the tea and pecked
at the biscuits.

The farmer reached out for his tea.
"Oh, the tea and biscuits," he cried.
"Lovely," clucked Hilda.
"Thank you so much."

And she went on her way.

"Just look," clucked Hilda.
"My friends have set the table for my
birthday tea. How wonderful."

She jumped up on to the table. All the
other hens joined her and Otto,
the cockerel, crowed, "Cock a doodle-do!
Happy Birthday to you!"

They all pecked eagerly at the crumbs.
And Hilda Hen clucked, "Thank you
everyone for my presents. I've had
a really happy birthday."

First published in Great Britain
in Gollancz Children's Paperbacks 1995
by Victor Gollancz
A Cassell imprint
Villiers House, 41/47 Strand, London WC2N 5JE

Copyright © Mary Wormell 1995

The right of Mary Wormell to be identified as author of this work
has been asserted by her in accordance with the Copyright,
Designs and Patents Act, 1988.

A catalogue record for this book is
available from the British Library

ISBN 0 575 05877 3

Printed in Hong Kong